Mighty Machines

Tugboats

by Matt Doeden

Consulting Editor: Gail Saunders-Smith, PhD

Consultant: Christopher Hall, President
Hall Associates of Washington, Inc.
Tugboat and Barge Brokerage

Capstone
press®

Mankato, Minnesota

Pebble Plus is published by Capstone Press,
151 Good Counsel Drive, P.O. Box 669, Mankato, Minnesota 56002.
www.capstonepress.com

1 2 3 4 5 6 12 11 10 09 08 07

Library of Congress Cataloging-in-Publication Data
Doeden, Matt.
    Tugboats / by Matt Doeden.
    p. cm.—(Pebble Plus. Mighty machines)
    Summary: "Summary: Simple text and photographs describe tugboats, their parts, and what they do"
—Provided by publisher.
    Includes bibliographical references and index.
    ISBN-13: 978-0-7368-6720-7 (hardcover)
    ISBN-10: 0-7368-6720-1 (hardcover)
    1. Tugboats—Juvenile literature. I. Title. II. Series.
VM464.D64 2007
386'.2232—dc22   2006027670

Editorial Credits
Mari Schuh, editor; Molly Nei, set designer; Patrick D. Dentinger, book designer; Jo Miller, photo researcher/
    photo editor

Photo Credits
Art Directors/Mike Insall, 18–19
Artemis Images, 1, 8–9
Corbis/Greg Smith, cover; Paul A. Souders, 13; Richard Cummins, 16–17; Tim Wright, 4–5;
    zefa/Wolfgang Deuter, 21
SuperStock/age fotostock, 14–15
Woodfin Camp & Associates Inc./Ed Zirkle, 7, 10–11

Note to Parents and Teachers

The Mighty Machines set supports national standards related to science, technology, and
society. This book describes and illustrates tugboats. The images support early readers
in understanding the text. The repetition of words and phrases helps early readers learn
new words. This book also introduces early readers to subject-specific vocabulary words,
which are defined in the Glossary section. Early readers may need assistance to read
some words and to use the Table of Contents, Glossary, Read More, Internet Sites, and
Index sections of the book.

Table of Contents

Tugboats 4

Parts of Tugboats. 6

What Tugboats Do. 14

Mighty Machines 20

Glossary 22

Read More 23

Internet Sites. 23

Index 24

Tugboats

Tugboats are little boats
with lots of power.
Tugboats help move
big ships and barges.

Parts of Tugboats

Tugboats have
big, strong engines.
The engine fills
most of the space
in a tugboat.

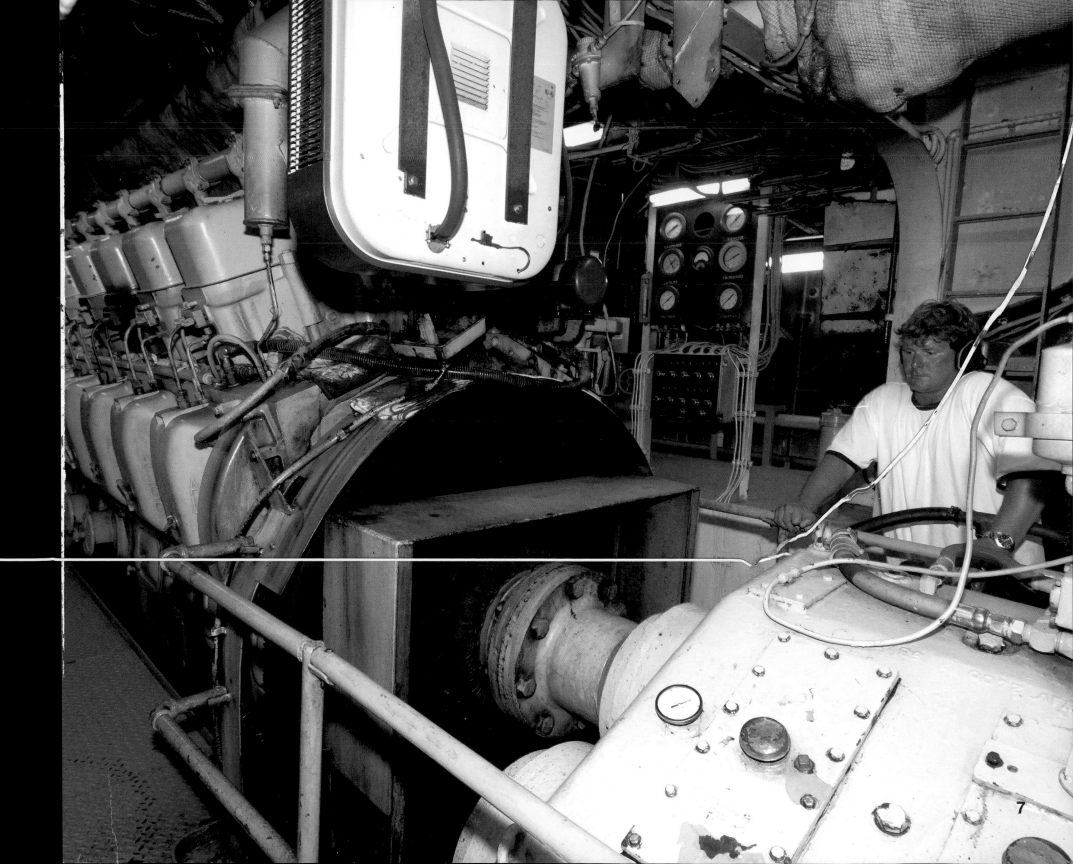

The engine turns
large propellers
under the tugboat.
These blades push tugboats
through the water.

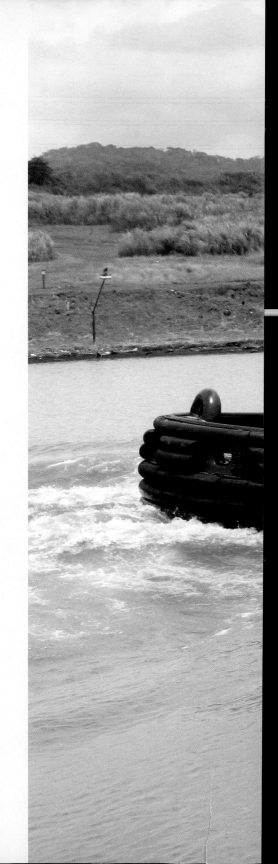

Thick ropes called towlines
tie tugboats to ships.

towline

The captain steers a tugboat

from the pilothouse.

13

What Tugboats Do

Tugboats help move big ships
in tight places.
Big ships can't turn easily
in narrow harbors and rivers.

Tugboats push ships.
Tugboats also can pull ships
with towlines.

Tugboats help
move ships into harbors.
Tugboats turn ships
to go back out to sea.

Mighty Machines

Tugboats are small,

but they are very strong.

Tugboats are

mighty machines.

21

Glossary

barge—a large, flat ship used to transport goods

captain—the person in charge of a boat or ship

engine—the part of a tugboat that powers the propeller

harbor—a place where ships unload their supplies

pilothouse—the room where the captain steers a tugboat

propeller—a set of spinning blades that pushes tugboats and other kinds of boats through water; propellers are found on the bottom side of tugboats.

towline—a rope that connects a tugboat to a ship or barge

Read More

Armentrout, David. *Ships.* Transportation. Vero Beach, Fla.: Rourke, 2004.

Schaefer, Lola M. *Tugboats.* The Transportation Library. Mankato, Minn.: Bridgestone Books, 2000.

Zuehlke, Jeffrey. *Tugboats.* Pull Ahead Books. Minneapolis: Lerner, 2007.

Internet Sites

FactHound offers a safe, fun way to find Internet sites related to this book. All of the sites on FactHound have been researched by our staff.

Here's how:

1. Visit *www.facthound.com*

2. Choose your grade level.

3. Type in this book ID **0736867201** for age-appropriate sites. You may also browse subjects by clicking on letters, or by clicking on pictures and words.

4. Click on the **Fetch It** button.

FactHound will fetch the best sites for you!

Index

barges, 4

captains, 12

engines, 6, 8

harbors, 14, 18

pilothouse, 12

power, 4

propellers, 8

pulling, 16

pushing, 8, 16

rivers, 14

sea, 18

ships, 4, 10, 14, 16, 18

size, 4, 20

steering, 12

strong, 6, 20

towlines, 10, 16

turning, 14, 18

water, 8

Word Count: 116
Grade: 1
Early-Intervention Level: 14